Collection
Stories from the kakawi

Gaële

the mysterious secret of the buttercups

written by
Sylvie Mathieu

illustrated by
Nick Boisvert

ROUTOUTOU

1030 St-Alexandre, Montréal (Québec) Canada H2Z 1P3

The kakawi is a very pretty duck who lives by the sea and very deep lakes. He is an excellent diver and can be found in many harbors, rummaging about near boats of all shapes and sizes. This is probably because of his keen interest in hearing stories of great voyages. Some people say it's because of the fishing, but we believe the kakawi has heard so many marvelous stories that he has now decided to share some of them with us.

And so we declare that anyone who tells a story is now called a 'kakawi'.

There are many different ways to ask someone for a story. However, to be told one of the kakawi's stories, you have to know 'the magic words'. You can ask any kakawi you like, big or small, young or old but a real kakawi will never, ever, tell a story without first hearing 'the words'.

And, since all kakawis love flattery, the more you say the magic words, the more they will tell you new stories.

The magic words are:

Kakawi! Kakawi!
Wise duck so fair and sweet
Pretty please, tell me
A story I can keep

To these words, the kakawi will always reply:

Of course!

Dawn

t all started . . .

...the morning Gaële crossed the little footbridge that spans the stony brook.

Soon she found herself in the valley of the daisies. As the sun rose, the great adventure began.

Gaële followed a path lined with wild, giant rushes and arrived at the top of the first hill. There she saw millions of tiny golden flowers chattering and bathing in the morning dew!

"Hello there and good morning to you," they called out cheerfully. "Who are you and just where do you think you're going?"

"Oh, hello, my name is Gaële and I'm looking for flowers that I can draw and learn about."

"Well, Gaële, we are the **buttercups** and we know a 'mysterious' secret. Bye-bye! Farewell! Ta-ta!"

"Huh! What secret? What do you mean 'mysterious'?"

"You'll find out later. Bye-bye! Farewell! Ta-ta!"

"But... but! When? How?"

But, but, buttercups!
Bye-bye! Farewell! Ta-ta!
No when, no how, no but
You'll find out soon enough
The 'shshh... secret'
...of the buttercups!

Still amazed by this first encounter, Gaële stopped to admire two very, very tall **lady's-slippers** when all of a sudden…

. . . she heard laughter!

"Hee-hee-hee-ho-ho-ho-ha-ha-ha!"

"Who's that? Who's laughing?"
asked Gaële.

"It's me! Me, me, me!"

"Who's ME?"

"YOU are Gaële. I am ME!"

"Then WHO are you?" she said
quite flustered.

"I'm Riki. Hee-hee-hee!"

"Riki hee hee hee?"

"No, just Riki," giggled a multicolored butterfly.
"Look up here."

Well, by then everyone was laughing—Gaële, the
two lady's-slippers and Riki, the laughing butterfly.

"And just where do you think
you're going?" asked Riki.

"I'm looking for flowers
that I can draw and
learn about."

"Well then, I'd better
come along with you."

Away they went and Gaële was very happy
to have a new friend joining the adventure.

It was lots of fun! Riki knew all the flowers by name. That made it easy for Gaële. She could ask the flowers to pose and draw them carefully in her notebook.

"Riki, do you know the secret of the buttercups?"

"Of course."

"Well, what is it?"

"Oh no, no, no! I can't tell you. It's a secret... a 'mysterious' secret!"

"But?!..."

To no avail.

Later, after reaching the top of the second hill, they came to a field of **pipsissewas**.

"Oh, how beautiful you are!
Soft and pink all over... Pink is
my favorite color. Hello, my
name is Gaële, what's yours?"

I'm Rosa
I'm Rosie
I'm Rosabella
Always one, two, three
Pretty tiny umbrellas
We're called the pipsissewas

"What lovely names. Can
I draw your picture?"

"Go right ahead,"
they answered.

The friendly pipsissewas
spread their petals and
bunched up next to
each other.

Gaële was pleased. Their
petals acted like parasols
and protected her
from the sun.

Noon

orning had gone by quickly...

...and Gaële was hungry. The sweet scent of clover blossoms made her stomach rumble.

Gaële sat down in the meadow to rest and eat her favorite snack of bread covered with chocolate spread and pineapple.

Galoo, gagaloo
Tiny and sweet, beautiful Gaële
Galoo, gagaloo
Lovely Gaële, doo doo doo doo

The grass and the clover around her was so tall, she could hardly be seen. Gaële was completely hidden! Riki searched for her here, there and everywhere calling:

"Gaële, gagaloo? Gaële...? Yoo-hoo, where are you?"

Laughing, Gaële crouched down even deeper in the grass, now totally out of sight! It was a neat trick.

"Well, that will teach you, little butterfly, to keep the secret of the buttercups from me," she chuckled to herself.

But later, when they came to a
field of **musk mallows**…

…it was Riki's turn to play a trick on Gaële. Each and every mallow of
the meadow was changing into a colorful butterfly and soon the
whole field was giggling and tickling her.

"Yoo-hoo, Gaële? Gagaloo…? Hee-hee-hee-ho-ho! Yoo-hoo?"

Right then and there, the playful butterflies rose up from the ground
and swept Gaële off her feet!

"But… Where are we going?"

"To see the flowers, of course," they replied.

And so Gaële was taken up into the air on the wings of laughing,
playful, magical and multicolored butterflies.

Now look at Gaële, see how she flies, carried

on the wings of the musk mallow butterflies!

Afternoon

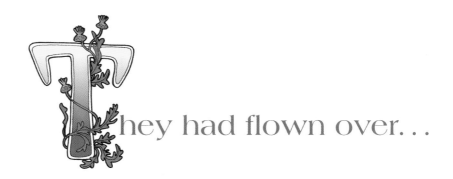

hey had flown over...

...a great big bunch of **bluebells** when the butterflies suddenly dropped her into one of the flowers.

These delicate flowers like to sway gently in the afternoon breeze and Riki laughed with glee while rocking back and forth.

"What fun! Whoopee! Hee-hee-hee! Yippee!"

But Gaële didn't think all this rocking and swaying was so much fun.

"Hum… You're all very pretty and nice but my tummy is feeling a bit queasy with all this rocking and rolling."

Just as she was wondering how to get herself out of this situation, she slipped and started to slide down, faster and faster, first on a petal, then on a leaf, down and down to suddenly find herself…

...flat on her stomach amongst the wintergreens!

"Oof! But where am I now?" she wondered.

For a moment, Gaële thought she was dreaming because all around her the wintergreens were singing in harmony.

Ding Ding Dong
We are the wintergreens
We like to sing this song
Do you know what it means?

"What new riddle is this? How can they sing like that?"

Gaële soon understood. Riki was flitting from bell to bell and making each one ring.

"Hum! This butterfly has more secrets and tricks up his sleeve than I ever thought possible," she reflected.

Dusk

t was getting late....

...and Gaële was getting a little tired. But before going home, the two friends wanted to watch the sun set over the pond. Gaële went up to a pretty blue flower and asked:

"Excuse me, but before you close for the night, would you please tell us how to get to the pond?"

"Of course, dear. Just follow the path, right through the woods."

"The woods? Oh my goodness! Well, thank you very much, you're very gentle and kind."

"Of course," answered the flower, "and by the way, we are the gentians."

Side by side, the 2 friends bravely…

...ventured through the woods.

When they arrived at the pond they were amazed to see **birdfoots**—who, as everyone knows are flowers!—reflecting in the water like so many setting suns.

Riki and Gaële clapped their hands in joy at such an enchanting sight.

To rest a while, Gaële lay down on the cushy leaf of a **marsh marigold**.

The golden flowers hung over her head like a starry roof.

She closed her eyes and drifted to sleep, carried away by the wondrous delights of the day.

Meanwhile, Riki was teasing the stars and making them giggle.

Their laughter was heard all over the Land of the Flowers.

It is said that many of them didn't sleep very well that night and that some looked a bit wilted the next morning.

But that's another story...

For now the kakawi declares...

...this story is done.

Flowers of the meadow
Butterflies in flight
Gaële is sleeping
Shshh... out like a light

– But... what about the secret?

– You mean... the 'mysterious' secret. We'll try to find it, the next time we go to the Land of the Flowers. Now, it's time for you to sleep.

A song for Gaële

Sweetest of the sweet, Gaële,
Sweet, a licorice treat
Buttercups and orchids of gold
Sweet, honey from the bees
Pipsissewas and winter's freeze
Gaële, my lovely Gaële

You smell like the flowers, Gaële,
Clover's perfume kissing the dusk
The soothing scent of purple musk
That butterflies like to tease
By tickling them under their leaves
Gaële, my lovely Gaële

Eensie, teensie, weensie Gaële,
Tiny as a scottish bluebell
The elliptical wintergreens
And the gentians along the trail
Fill your dreams of wonderful tales
Gaële, my lovely Gaële

Nighty-night, sleep tight, Gaële,
Peaceful dreams, sleep well
Little birdfoot, time for bed
Soft marigold, rest your head
I'm here, watching over you well
Beautiful dreams, Gaële,
My lovely Gaële,
...Sweet lovely Gaële

Refrain:

Galoo, gagaloo
Tiny and sweet, beautiful Gaële
Galoo, gagaloo
Lovely Gaële
Doo doo doo doo

Pipsissewa *(common)*

In Greek, the name means "who loves winter." The American Indians used to make a potion with the roots to relieve rheumatic pains. It is especially pretty when it opens in July and August. Petite, it rarely grows higher than 12 inches.

Common names:
Prince's pine
Winter's freeze

Botanical name:
Chimaphila umbellata

Yellow Lady's-slipper

This tall orchid can grow up to 20 inches. It smells nice. A real northerner, it prefers the damp woods of Asian, European and American mountains. Overly collected, it is more and more difficult to find and in many countries is protected by law.

Common name:
Little shoe

Botanical name:
Cypripedium parviflorum

Red Clover

These beautiful crimson flowers are very fragrant and attract many insects, but their nectar is located so deep that only the insects with very long proboscis manage to harvest some, like the butterflies for example.

Common names:
Big clover
Prairie clover

Botanical name:
Trifolium pratense

Shinleaf *(elliptical)*

Here is a real North American. It has attractive, mat, sweet-smelling and pale-pink blossoms. This is one of my favorite flowers.

Common names:
Wintergreen
Lily-of-the-valley

Botanical name:
Pyrola elliptica

Bluebell

The pastel blue corollas of this pretty flower sway to the slightest breeze. It seems very fragile but actually is a sturdy rockery plant.

Common names:
Harebell
Bellflower
Bluebell of Scotland

Botanical name:
Campanula rotundifolia

anthology

Musk Mallow

This pretty flower managed to escape from the grand gardens of European properties and spread through our fields and our valleys. It must be very ancient because some seeds have been found at prehistoric sites.

Common names:
Little cheese
Musk rose

Botanical name:
Malva moschata

Buttercup *(common)*

Buttercups can be found everywhere, in fields and meadows, on mountain-tops and in valleys. They are a part of our lives. While considered a weed by many, for most of us it remains an image of summer.

Common names:
Butter flower
Crowfoot
Gold cup

Botanical name:
Ranunculus acris

Birdfoot

Its real name is *Bird's-foot trefoil*. This is another beautiful plant brought to America by Europeans who used it as cattle feed. It grows erratically in any soil but really prefers damp areas and marshes.

Common names:
Pea flower
Lotus

Botanical name:
Lotus corniculatus

Marsh Marigold *(yellow)*

Its Latin name, *Caltha*, comes from Greek which means basket. In the old days, the roots were boiled to prepare an ointment used to cure cuts and scratches.

Common names:
Cowslip
King-cup
Water-blobs

Botanical name:
Caltha palustris

Gentian *(fringed)*

This gentian looks like a beautiful vase of multiple shades of blue. It grows late in the fall and likes to live in clearings and at the edge of woodlands.

Botanical name:
Gentiana crinita

Dear Gaële
Today I discovered
a new bird.
I tried to talk with him but
he did not understand.
Here is a drawing I made.
Do you know who
he is?

I think he
comes from a
faraway
country
and I decided
to give him a hat
so he would not catch cold.
I also met a strange butterfly who
laughs all the time....
he says he knows you!!
Is it true?

over→